JULIET™

THE JUMPSTART SQUAD

BY

JULIE DRISCOLL

COVER ART BY KRISTI VALIANT
STORY ILLUSTRATIONS BY TRISH ROUELLE

An Our Generation® *book*

BATTAT INCORPORATED *Publisher*

A very special thanks to the editor,
Joanne Burke Casey.

Our Generation® Books is a registered trademark of Battat Incorporated.
Text copyright © 2010 by Julie Driscoll
Characters portrayed in this book are fictitious. Any references to historical
events, real people, or real locales are used fictitiously. Other names,
chararacters, places, and incidents are products of the author's imagination,
and any resemblance to actual events or locales or persons, living or dead,
is entirely coincidental.
ISBN: 978-0-9794542-7-1
Printed in China

For Dad and Shirley

Read all the adventures in the
Our Generation® Book Series

One Smart Cookie
featuring Hally™

Blizzard on Moose Mountain
featuring Katelyn™

Stars in Your Eyes
featuring Sydney Lee™

The Note in the Piano
featuring Mary Lyn™

The Mystery of the Vanishing Coin
featuring Eva™

Adventures at Shelby Stables
featuring Lily Anna™

The Sweet Shoppe Mystery
featuring Jenny™

The Jumpstart Squad
featuring Juliet™

CONTENTS

Chapter One   Finding My Thing   Page 9

Chapter Two   Sticking It Out   Page 15

Chapter Three   Boom!   Page 20

Chapter Four   Getting Psyched Up   Page 29

Chapter Five   Having a Ball   Page 37

Chapter Six   The Competition   Page 41

Chapter Seven   Striving to Be My Best   Page 44

Chapter Eight   Seeing Clearly   Page 48

Chapter Nine   One, Two, Three...   Page 54

Chapter Ten   Whatever!   Page 59

Chapter Eleven   Do Your Thing   Page 71

Chapter Twelve   Off to States!   Page 79

Chapter Thirteen   S-U-C-C-E-S-S   Page 83

EXTRA! EXTRA! READ ALL ABOUT IT!
Big words, wacky words, powerful words, funny words...
*what do they all mean? They are marked with this symbol * .*
Look them up in the Glossary at the end of this book.

Chapter One

FINDING MY THING

The brightly lit gymnasium was filled with every noise imaginable. People were shouting, feet were stomping, hands were clapping. And the loud music that was booming through the large clunky speakers surrounding the performance area echoed through my body so that I couldn't even feel my own heart beating.

A banner with the words: DETERMINATION, DRIVE, STRIVE...TO BE YOUR VERY BEST, hung on a wall above the bleachers.

But all of it was a big blur to me as I was raised up into my pyramid stunt. I followed with my high-V pose and a big, nervous smile.

My next two moves were the defining moments for me and the entire Park Valley Rangers junior cheerleading squad. It was what we had all worked so hard for. And it all came down to me and two other girls.

It was pretty amazing—to be where I was at that point in

time, balancing on Nicole's shoulders, wearing my pink uniform with the light blue pleats and navy stripes running through it... my hair done up perfectly in two pigtails and lots of hairspray... trying my very hardest not to fall.

So much had happened in the past year. And even though I had come so far I still had my doubts. Perhaps I wasn't good enough. What if I messed up?

Before I tell you what happened next, I should probably explain how I got there in the first place. So, here's my story. Here's what led me to that critical* point...

ॐ ॐ

It all began when I complained to my best friend, Monica, that I'd never find anything that I was truly good at. For one reason or another, nothing seemed to stick.

First, I tried softball. It was OK. I especially didn't mind the part when the coach stuck me way out in right field. I'd purposely stay far enough back, near the tall pine trees that lined the chainlink fence, so that hardly any fly balls would come my way.

And that was a very good thing for me because I could just stand there and daydream or play with the tiny little inchworms that floated by on almost invisible strings. I loved catching them in my hand and then watching as they crept along my palm, scrunching their tiny green bodies into the shape of a small, cursive letter "n" and flattening out again.

Then, of course, once in a while—PLUNK! A ball would drop to the ground near where I was standing. The crowd would usually groan a bit. My dad would yell, "Juliet, pick it up and throw it!" So I would. I'd throw the ball as best I could. It would travel only a short distance and another girl would have to run and retrieve* it from the grass.

Well, anyhow, I think you get the picture. Softball—not my thing!

After my attempt at softball, Monica, being the best friend that she is, made me try soccer. Soccer is definitely *her* thing and she's really good at it. Her dad is a coach so it was no surprise when I conveniently ended up on the same team as her.

I tried to enjoy it. And I hoped it would become my *thing*. But all that running up and down the field, and not being able to use your hands…. As it turned out, soccer wasn't really my thing, either.

Monica was disappointed, but she quickly decided to make it her mission to help me find something that I *was* good at.

It was nearing the end of the school year. We were copying our weekly spelling words from the board. One of the words was "perfection." I paused and thought about that word for a moment. *How nice it would be to be perfect at something.* I pictured myself being so good at something that everyone was smiling at me and clapping....

"Here! Take one and pass it back!" Monica interrupted my thoughts as she placed a stack of bright blue paper on my desk. I hadn't finished copying my words.

I took a piece of paper from the top of the stack and passed the rest back to Eddie, the boy behind me. Then I quickly finished jotting down the last three words on the board.

Monica turned back around to face me. I glanced up and noticed she was wearing her excited expression— big smile, no teeth showing, eyebrows raised and eyes bugging out of her head. "Juliet! Now this is something you should try," she said excitedly.

The big bold letters that read "PARK VALLEY RANGERS JUNIOR CHEERLEADING" stood out clearly against the brightly colored paper. But the smaller words below it were a bit fuzzy.

"Me? A cheerleader?" I raised one eyebrow.

"Yes, you! You're a good dancer, remember?" Monica was referring to the summer that we took hip-hop* classes together. That actually wasn't bad and I *was* pretty good at it.

"And there are no balls to catch or kick—just pompoms," she joked.

I squinted and again tried to read the smaller words on the page but they were still a bit blurry. "I can't read what it says below."

Monica read my flier upside down from where she sat. "It says, SIGN UPS THIS THURSDAY AT THE PARK VALLEY ELEMENTARY GYMNASIUM.

"Take this home and show it to your parents," Monica commanded in an assertive* tone.

I sighed and tucked the paper into my folder.

And as you probably guessed by now, that's what led me to become a Park Valley Rangers junior cheerleader—that bright blue flier, my best friend Monica and my quest* to find something that I was good at.

Chapter Two

STICKING IT OUT

The other cheerleaders and I sat on the cold, damp grass waiting for our practice to begin. I zipped up my hooded warm-up jacket as far as it would go and tucked my bare, goose-bumped knees up under it.

The older, high school varsity* cheerleaders who occupied* a nearby section of the football field had already begun practicing. I admired them. They appeared so confident and sure of themselves.

The junior football players were at the far end of the field performing jumping jacks in unison*. Every now and again they'd let out a loud grunt.

The high school football players seemed like giants compared to the junior squad as they jogged by in their big, bulky uniforms. Chuck, my brother Aiden's former best friend, noticed me and waved.

I didn't recognize him at first under all that football

armor*. But I knew it was him when he shouted "Hey Pip!" I waved back.

Pip is short for pip-squeak. That's what he always called me.

I missed Chuck. Even though he lives right next door I hadn't seen him around much anymore.

A few years ago Aiden, Chuck and their friend Bandana formed a band. They called themselves the Ultimatums and practiced in our garage all the time. Aiden plays guitar, Bandana is the drummer and Chuck *was* the singer. Soon after, they added a guitarist, Splinter, and another guy, Mike, who plays the keyboard*.

The Ultimatums actually weren't that bad. Once in a while they'd even let me and Monica hang out with them, as long as we'd bring them snacks and promise not to make too much noise.

But ever since Chuck made the high school football team, he and Aiden have hardly spoken. I think my brother resents Chuck because he no longer has time to hang out with the band anymore. Now that the Ultimatums don't have a singer they just sort of make loud, annoying noises with their instruments and goof around a lot.

I was officially a Park Valley Rangers junior cheerleader. There were fifteen girls on our squad. We didn't have to try out or anything. However, I quickly discovered that automatically making the team didn't mean it was going to be easy.

Since the sign-ups last spring I'd put more time and effort into cheering than any other sport. We practiced a good part of the summer to help us prepare for the upcoming Regionals*. And most of the girls on the team, including me, attended a summer cheer camp to improve our skills even further.

So far I liked it OK. But up until that point, all I'd been doing was cheering and cheering some more. I was getting pretty good at it but it was a lot of work.

Olivia, our team captain, who's been with the squad for four years now, told me that cheerleading gets really fun and exciting once the pep rallies and competitions begin. I sure hoped so.

Summer was also when I found out I needed to wear eyeglasses. I was particularly having trouble reading things up close. I didn't like wearing them much but I had them in

my gym bag just in case.

"We'll be practicing in the gymnasium next week," said Lexie, one of my teammates, as she rubbed her hands together and looked around for our coach.

"That's good," I said. "Otherwise, I'm going to have to start packing my earmuffs and mittens in my gym bag."

Lexie and I met over the summer at cheer camp. She's new to the squad, just like me.

Olivia finally arrived along with our coach, Mrs. Garcia. Olivia pulled Theodora, a small stuffed bear, from her bag and perched her on the grass so that she was resting against her tall, steel water bottle.

Theodora is our team's mini mascot—a smaller version of Theo, the real, life-sized bear mascot that performs with the high school cheerleading squad. She wears a cheerleading uniform similar to ours except hers is much smaller.

Each year Theodora is passed down to the girl on the squad who works the hardest and shows the most dedication*. Olivia says she brings the squad spirit and good luck. I just think she's a really cute stuffed bear.

This year, Olivia got Theodora. And she deserved it, too. She was the perfect cheerleader—perfect in every way. Her long strawberry blond hair that never seemed out of place, her pretty smile, her kind personality and her exceptional cheerleading skills all added up to perfect.

"OK," said Mrs. Garcia, "everyone get into formation*."

We all stood and took our places on the grass.

I took a deep breath. Another cheerleading practice— another day of figuring out what I was good at—*and* whether or not I had what it took to stick it out.

Chapter Three

BOOM!

Because there were so many of us on the squad, Mrs. Garcia divided our team into three smaller groups to work on cheerleading-related activities such as making signs and passing out fliers.

Four girls from the squad, Olivia, Nicole, Lisa and Lexie, met at my house after school one day to make signs for the upcoming pep rally.

Pep rallies are a big deal in Park Valley. They help get everyone in the town psyched up for a winning season. In fact, I was quickly discovering that anything related to football, including cheerleading, seems to be a big deal in our town. It's all about winning—and not just games, either. Cheerleading competitions are a huge deal, too.

The cheerleading coaches take their jobs very seriously. Three years ago, the high school cheerleaders made it all the way to States*. If they had won at States they would have gone on to Nationals*—a televised event that takes place in Florida. It's one of the highest honors in cheerleading.

It was an unusually warm day for fall, which was a good thing because the signs we were working on were so big. We needed a wide-open space, like my driveway, to set up shop. Monica came over to hang out with us and help before her soccer practice. She lives down the street and was already friendly with a few of the girls on my squad.

The only downfall to working outside in the driveway was the fact that we were right beside the garage. And even though the garage door and windows were closed we could still hear the aggravating twanging of my brother Aiden's guitar, mixed with the BANG, BANG, BOOM sounds that Bandana was making on the drums.

Sometimes, when all the band members were present and they weren't goofing around, the Ultimatums sounded pretty good. On this particular day, however, I got the impression that they were making annoying noises just to irritate me and my friends.

Theodora was the only one that seemed oblivious* to the clatter coming from the garage. She sat quietly under the cherry tree beside the garage and smiled at us as we worked.

BANG, STRUM, TWANG, BOOM! Some of the girls started giggling.

I shook my head and tried to focus on our banner. The letters I was painting were large enough so that I didn't need to wear my eyeglasses. And that was a good thing because I'd left them in my desk at school. I didn't like wearing them much. It was just one more thing for me to remember.

One day in class, before a spelling test, I snuck them out from inside my desk and put them on. Andrea, the girl beside me, noticed immediately. She told me that I looked so cute and smart. Then Eddie, who's a big tease, began calling me "four eyes."

Since then, I've tried to get along without them. BANG, BOOM, TWANG!!

"That's it!" I stood and tiptoed over the jars of opened paint.

The noises got even louder when I opened the side door to the garage, then came to an abrupt* halt* as soon as Aiden and Bandana noticed me standing in the doorway.

"Juliet, can't you read?" asked Aiden.

He could tell I didn't have a clue as to what he was talking about.

"The sign, dummy! It says KEEP OUT. And that means you, too!"

I turned. Hanging on the open door beside me was a *new*, wooden sign with small letters etched* in black. I could only make out the word OUT.

"Aiden, you guys are bothering us with those stupid noises. Either play something that makes sense or don't play at all!" I shouted at him.

"We're just warming up while we wait for the other guys," explained Bandana who had chosen to wear a yellow bandana around his neck on that particular day. Bandana had an entire collection of bandanas—a color for every day of the week—or so it seemed.

His real name is Bob Hannah. But because he plays in a band and his last name is Hannah, Splinter nicknamed him Band-ana.

Bandana used to play hockey with Aiden. That's how they met. Aiden told me that, due to an injury, he couldn't play sports anymore. That's one of the reasons the guys formed the band in the first place. It gave Bandana something to do. And it quickly became their *thing* to do together.

Just then I heard a faint rumbling noise followed by loud clapping of wood against pavement. I stepped out of the garage and saw Splinter and Mike rolling up the driveway on their skateboards.

"Watch out for the wet paint and signs!" I warned as they glided closer.

Mike steered his skateboard up onto the grass. Splinter kicked the back end of his board with his heel. It popped up in the air. Then he grabbed it with his hand. His skateboard was a peculiar design with a strange looking, bluish-green monster on it. The monster had three eyes and webbed feet that were almost as big as its head.

Mike and Splinter paused to admire our signs. "GO PARK VALLEY RANGERS! How original," joked Mike.

"What's with the cute little stuffed bear?" asked Splinter, as he weaved through the maze of paints and brushes and made his way toward Theodora.

Aiden appeared at the garage doorway, his guitar still slung* around his neck. Bandana stepped out as well.

"That's our mascot," replied Olivia. "She brings us luck."

"Too bad you guys don't have a real mascot like the high school team," joked Bandana.

"Yeah," added Aiden. "Instead they get this stupid little stuffed bear."

"Her name is Theodora," I shot back. "And don't call her stupid!"

Splinter picked up Theodora and tossed her across the driveway to Mike. "Boom!" he shouted. Boom was Splinter's favorite word. Almost everything he said had the word "boom" at the end of it.

"Go long!" yelled Mike as he tossed the bear over to Bandana.

"Stop it!" I cried.

Some of the girls began shouting and Olivia seemed pretty upset.

Aiden had Theodora again. He took a few steps back and tossed Theodora like a football. I darted toward him but he quickly fired her back across the driveway in Splinter's direction. This time Theodora sailed right over Splinter's head and landed squarely on one of the branches in the tree beside the garage.

"Whoops," joked Aiden. He and his friends began howling at the sight of Theodora in the tree.

"Boom!" laughed Splinter.

The girls and I ran over to the tree. Theodora was wedged in a branch high up out of our reach. She was facing downward, smiling at the ground.

"Aiden, get our mascot out of the tree or I'm going to get Mom," I demanded.

But he was too busy showing off in front of his friends. He began strumming a silly song on his guitar.

"Watch that bear up in the tree, hope it doesn't fall on me..."

Monica picked up her soccer ball and tried to dislodge*
Theodora from the tree but she didn't budge. Olivia and
the other girls stood by helplessly. I could feel my face
getting red with anger.

Just then a car door slammed. I noticed Chuck walking
up his driveway next door. He was wearing his football
uniform and carrying his helmet under his arm.

Bandana nodded to Chuck as if to say hello. Chuck
nodded back. Aiden turned abruptly and walked back
into the garage.

Chuck could see that my friends and I were upset.
"What's going on, Pip?" he asked me as he came closer.

I pointed to Theodora and explained what had
happened.

"Here, I'll give you a boost." He dropped his helmet
and cupped his hands so I could step onto them. Then he
raised me up.

I could barely reach her but I stretched my arms out as
long as they would go and jiggled the branch. Theodora
rolled off the branch and tumbled to the grass below.

Olivia swooped her up and brushed the leaves and dirt
from her fur.

"Thanks," I said, once my feet were firmly on the
ground again.

"You're welcome, Pip."

Chuck glanced over at the garage. The Ultimatums were already back inside making loud clanging noises.

He picked up his football helmet and stared into it for a moment. I got the sense that he missed hanging out with my brother and being part of the band.

"See you around," Chuck said, as he gazed over at the garage one more time. Then he turned and walked away.

Chapter Four

GETTING PSYCHED UP

On the day of the rally, all the cheerleaders wore their uniforms to school. The football players dressed in their football jerseys and many of the students had on the team colors—blue and white.

Olivia was right! Pep rallies were really fun and exciting. In fact, the entire day was exciting. The banner we had painted hung at the entranceway to the school. And everyone seemed to have more spirit than usual. Even Monica, who's usually not fully awake until lunchtime, appeared more bubbly and cheerful that day.

After school, all the football players and cheerleaders boarded busses to be taken over to the high school where the rally was being held. We waved out the windows, shaking our pompoms at the parents and students as our bus drove out the school's circular driveway and headed across town.

When we arrived at the high school we all waited in a quiet hallway behind two heavy swinging doors while students and parents filed into the gymnasium.

The high school cheerleaders were there as well. Many of them commented on how cute we looked. Sophie, the high school cheer captain, reminisced* about the days when she was once our age.

Sophie was a big hugger. She skipped around the hallway hugging her squad mates, wishing them all good luck.

When Theo, the real, life-sized mascot, appeared in the hallway Sophie rushed over to him and wrapped her arms around his big wooly body.

"Look girls," Sophie said. She swung Theo around to face Olivia, Lexie and me. "This is our mysterious mascot, Theo!"

He bowed to each of us and then gave us all high-fives.

"Who's under there?" Lexie asked as Theo strutted* off.

"It's a secret," said Sophie. "This year our squad didn't have a mascot. No one seemed to want the job. Finally someone came forward and agreed to do it as long as they could remain anonymous*. Our coach is the only person who knows who it is."

Theo wore blue striped shorts and a football jersey similar to the one the football players wore. He was certainly a lot bigger than our mascot. Which reminded me...

"Olivia, where's Theodora?" I asked.

She smiled at Lexie and me. "Come on, I'll show you guys."

We crept back through the swinging doors and down the hall toward the gymnasium.

When I peeked through the rectangular glass window I gasped. The high school gymnasium was noticeably bigger than the one at our school and the bleachers that lined the walls were filled to the top with people.

Monica had drawn a sign in art class that said "GO JULIET!" She was planning to hold it up for me during our performance. I knew she and Aiden were somewhere in the crowd but it was like looking for a needle in a haystack to find them.

It was also very loud. There were so many people talking all at once. Up to that point I hadn't been nervous, but I was quickly beginning to feel the butterflies in my stomach.

Olivia pointed to the far wall near the scoreboard. Theodora was balancing contentedly* on one of the blue backboard cushions. She looked so small and adorable. "That's where we'll sit when we're done performing," Olivia explained.

Just then the rest of the cheerleaders came barreling down the hallway.

"It's almost time to go on," Lisa said excitedly.

We formed into a single line and waited quietly. We could hear the principal addressing the crowd over the loudspeaker.

The high school girls got in line behind us.

"Let's do this!" said Sophie. Then she high-fived Theo and her squad mates.

Theo noticed that some of the girls on my squad and I seemed nervous. He tried to keep us calm by doing a little tap dance and shaking his tail.

A few moments later—loud applause and stomping sounds. The next thing I knew, the doors were flung open and we were running out to the center of the gymnasium.

STOMP, STOMP, CLAP…. The crowd began banging on the bleachers while we formed two lines. An announcer's voice echoed over a loudspeaker as he called out the junior football players' names. They ran between our formation and then took their seats in a reserved* section of the bleachers.

Some of the older students had painted their faces blue and white. They stood up and shouted out the players' names along with us. Other kids were waving signs that said "RANGERS RULE" and "GO PARK VALLEY!!"

After the junior football players were announced, we performed our routine. Because Lisa, Brenna and I were the smallest girls on our team we were the flyers—the girls who stood on the top of the pyramids.

Nicole was the base and Lexie and Dee were my spotters. When they went to lift me up I fumbled a bit and I was way behind the other flyers as I was raised up into my half-extension liberty stunt.

From the top of the pyramid, I glanced out into the crowd. I saw lots of smiling faces, hands clapping and feet stomping. I spotted the sign that said "GO JULIET!" It made me smile knowing Monica was there, rooting for me.

We followed up our cheer performance with a quick dance routine and a big bow. The crowd applauded. Then we ran over and took our places on the floor below the scoreboard.

When the high school cheerleaders came out, the crowd cheered even louder, especially when their mascot entered. Theo gave everyone a victory sign and did a little dance. He was very entertaining.

I didn't think it could get any noisier in the gymnasium, but it did. When the high school football players were announced the crowd went wild. The town of Park Valley was officially psyched up for the season!

Like I said before—it was a very exciting day! If only I hadn't messed up on my liberty stunt. I realized that I needed to practice extra hard so I wouldn't mess up next time.

Yep, everything went well—that is, until Theodora went missing.

At the end of the rally, Theodora was no longer balancing on the blue backboard cushion near the scoreboard, smiling contentedly.

She was nowhere to be found!

Chapter Five

HAVING A BALL

The following day was the first Park Valley Rangers junior football game. It was a cold, dreary day so I packed my earmuffs and mittens in my gym bag in case I needed them.

The entire squad was sad about the disappearance of Theodora. Olivia seemed the most upset. We all tried to make her feel better. Lisa brought her a piece of her favorite chocolate. Monica and I drew her a picture of a smiley face with lots of hearts on it. And Brenna brought her a cheerleading magazine.

None of us had any clue as to who could have taken Theodora. So many people had come and gone that afternoon. We were all so wrapped up in our cheering that we weren't paying much attention. It wasn't until after most of the people had filed out of the gymnasium that Olivia remembered Theodora and went to retrieve her from the backboard. That's when she noticed she wasn't there.

During the football game our squad cheered to the people in the bleachers. We shouted through our megaphones and got them all to cheer along with us.

My favorite cheer was the one about success:

S-U-C-C-E-S-S
That's the way we spell SUCCESS
V-I-C-T-O-R-Y
VICTORY, VICTORY—that's our cry
R-A-N-G-E-R-S
RANGERS, RANGERS—we're the best
S-U-C-C-E-S-S
SUCCESS…VICTORY…RANGERS!

Then, at halftime, we ran over to the visitors' side of the field to welcome the cheerleaders and introduce ourselves.

BOURNE BRONCOS HERE'S TO YOU, WITH A BIG HELLO AND A HOW DO YOU DO…

When the game finally ended I felt tired and hungry.

"I think you guys are in pretty good shape for the competition next weekend," Mrs. Garcia told us as we walked over to a bench to collect our gym bags. *I sure hope so*, I thought. I'd never worked so hard in my life.

Mrs. Garcia was referring to the regional competition*—a particularly important day for our squad. Winning at Regionals would qualify our squad for the state competition. The Park Valley Rangers junior cheerleading squad had never made it to States before.

As I was zipping up my gym bag I noticed an envelope lying on the ground beside one of Olivia's pompoms. Written on the front of the envelope were the words: "Jumpstart Squad." *What's a Jumpstart Squad?* I thought.

"Here Olivia," I said. I picked up the envelope and held it out for her. "I think this is for us."

She was busy packing up her things. "Can you read what it says?" she asked me.

I opened it up and I think I startled everyone around me, including myself, when I let out a giant SHRIEK!

Inside was a photograph of Theodora. She was leaning

on a water fountain, smiling as she always does, and wearing sunglasses that were way too big for her face. To her right was a beach ball. To her left was a sign that I could barely read.

The other girls on the squad gathered around me. They all shrieked, too, when they saw the photograph.

"That's the fountain in the center of town," said Lexie.

"Yeah," said Brenna. "There's the town hall and the tall bronzed* statue of a man in the background."

"What does the sign say?" I asked.

"Having a ball!" said Lexie.

Olivia was speechless. We couldn't believe our eyes.

A prankster had taken our team mascot.

Chapter Six

THE COMPETITION

An entire week had passed since we received the photo of Theodora, however my squad mates and I didn't have a lot of time to give it much thought. We were all too busy practicing for the upcoming regional competition. And that day came and went so fast that my head was spinning.

When my mom, dad, and I arrived home from Regionals I ran upstairs to my bedroom to call Monica. I couldn't wait to tell her all about it. Our squad had placed third. That meant we qualified for States. The Park Valley junior cheerleaders had never made it that far before.

"It was unbelievable!" I told Monica as I kicked off my shoes and plopped my head on my pillow. "We were all so good."

Monica was happy for me. "It looks like your hard

work has finally paid off," she said.

She was right. It had. All those long hours in the gymnasium, practicing my toe touches and pike jumps until I had them down cold. I'd been working my absolute hardest to get my moves perfect.

"Everyone was so nervous. But it was too bad Theodora wasn't with us," I sighed.

"Yeah, if only you could figure out who took her," said Monica.

I explained to Monica how it was close, though, and we almost didn't make it. When I went to do my liberty stunt I was a little shaky. I was certain the judges noticed. *I still need to work on that*, I thought.

Our squad was in fourth place. But then, the team ahead of us got eliminated. Dropping down to your knees without placing your hands down first looked like a small enough mistake to me. But according to the competition rules it was a safety violation and they were disqualified*. That moved us up to third place and qualified us for States.

My phone beeped. "Hold on," I said to Monica,

"I have another call." I hit the talk button on my phone. "Hello?"

"Juliet. It's Lexie. Guess what?" She sounded panicky*.

"What?"

"You're not going to believe this! Olivia just received another photograph of Theodora. Someone left it in her mailbox."

"Hold on," I told her. I hit the talk button again. "Monica...I'm going to have to call you back!"

Chapter Seven

STRIVING TO BE MY BEST

It seemed like the school day would never end, and I was more than anxious to get to practice so I could see the latest picture of Theodora. When the school bell sounded I dashed to the girls' locker room and dressed quickly in my training shorts and top.

My cheer shoes were still untied as I rushed into the gymnasium. Lisa and a few other girls from the squad were hovering* in a circle, studying the new photograph.

"Look," said Lexie when she saw me approaching. "Theodora was at Bent's Cream and Cone." She held out the photo so I could see it.

"Yeah, and she had a Frosty Frizzle," said Brenna.

Theodora was leaning against a napkin holder on top of a table. I couldn't read the small print, but the red and yellow stripes on the menu to her right, and similarly colored Frosty Frizzle cup to her left, were good indications* that she was in fact at Bent's Cream and Cone.

"What does it say below?" I asked.

"Just chillin'," said Olivia.

Dee began to giggle. "At least she's having fun."

"Yeah," said Brenna. "But do you think they'll eventually give her back?"

"I hope so," said Olivia. "I miss her." She paused and then her expression turned to anger. "And when I find out

just chillin'

45

who took her…"

A door slammed. We looked up and saw Mrs. Garcia. She was all smiles as she walked toward us.

"First," she began, "I want to tell you all how proud I am of you and what a wonderful job you did yesterday. But…if you want a shot at States you need to be better than just good. That means adding a few more practices during the week *and* incorporating* some more complicated stunts into your routine. Are you all up for that?"

We looked around at each other and nodded yes.

"Also," Mrs. Garcia continued, "there are several costs associated with competing at States such as the entry fee, bus and hotel expenses. And we'll need chaperones. To help pay for all this we're going to have to do some fundraising*.

"I checked with the school and they agreed to allow us to host a pancake breakfast in the cafeteria before one of the football games. In addition, we'll have to do some canning—lots of canning."

"What's canning?" I whispered to Brenna.

"That's when you stand outside a store with a sign

and ask people to donate money," she answered.

"OK girls," said Mrs. Garcia, "everyone get into position. We have a lot of work ahead of us!"

I knew that the next few weeks were going to be all about cheerleading and fundraising. But I didn't mind. I leapt to my spot, ready and eager to work even harder than before.

Before I became a cheerleader, I just wanted to find something that I was good at. This time, I wanted to be better than good—this time, I wanted to win!

Chapter Eight

SEEING CLEARLY

The doorbell rang. I ran to the front door and opened it. Monica's face was hidden behind an oversized, fluffy, yellow pillow. It was balancing on top of all her other sleepover stuff—sleeping bag, overnight bag and her favorite snack, Twisty Crisps.

"A little help?" she asked.

I grabbed the pillow and the bag of Twisty Crisps.

"Don't open those yet," she warned me, knowing that I loved Twisty Crisps just as much as she did.

Olivia, Lisa, Nicole and Lexie hadn't arrived yet. They were probably taking a little rest after our long day of canning. It was, in fact, a long two weeks of canning. But we were finally done.

Standing outside and asking for donations wasn't as easy as I thought it would be. And I didn't know which hurt more: my feet from standing for so long—or my cheeks from smiling so much.

Our group was assigned to Charlie's Corner Market. Most of the time we worked in shifts so that we could cover a large part of the day without having to stay the entire time. But I usually ended up sticking around for most of it because I felt like the girls needed my help.

I got pretty good at canning, too. Many of the people we spoke to seemed interested in our cause and were happy to donate a little something. Some people were a little grumpy, though. I found that if I told a joke or smiled my biggest smile, I'd get a better response.

I'd finally decided to wear my eyeglasses. I realized that if I wanted to be my very best it would probably be a good idea if I could see what I was doing. The only time I didn't really need

them was when I was sleeping or cheering.

A lot of familiar faces came and went from Charlie's Corner Market. At first, some people didn't recognize me with my new eyeglasses. Others commented on how cute and stylish I looked.

As a reward for all our hard work and for wearing my eyeglasses, my mom and dad had agreed to let me have a sleepover.

During that two-week period Olivia had also received another photograph of Theodora. The prankster had taken her to the West Park Movie Theater in town to see the movie, *Globule Heroes*. In the photo, Theodora was wearing 3D

glasses and balancing a bag of popcorn on her lap.

We pretty much assumed that she had seen *Globule Heroes* because it was the only movie in town being shown in 3D. We were all beginning to wonder how long these pranks would go on for and whether or not the pranksters would return Theodora when they were done.

Monica and I went into the family room to set up our sleeping bags.

BANG, BOOM, TWANG!

I shook my head. It seemed that no matter where I went in my house I couldn't escape the noise from the Ultimatums. It never bothered me before, but now that I was no longer allowed in the garage it was just plain annoying.

Olivia, Nicole, Lisa and Lexie eventually arrived. We sat around eating pizza, popcorn and Twisty Crisps and talking about the upcoming competition. *How amazing it would be to win*, I thought.

Everything appeared to be going well. Even the Ultimatums cooperated by playing decent sounding music for a change. Mike had taken over Chuck's role as singer. He wasn't as good as Chuck but he was still OK.

The girls and I practiced our cheers. We made up a dance routine to one of the Ultimatums' songs. Monica was getting pretty good at cheering and dancing, too, except she wasn't very good at splits. Nicole sat on the floor with Monica and tried to straighten out her back leg.

"Maybe *I* should be your team mascot," Monica joked.

"Yeah," said Lisa, "especially because ours is missing."

"Speaking of which, do you have the pictures with you? I haven't seen them yet." Monica asked Olivia.

"Yeah," said Olivia. "They're in my bag."

Olivia grabbed the photos from the front pocket of her overnight bag while Monica untwisted her leg and rubbed it to get the circulation back.

We spread the photos out on the floor and studied them. Monica laughed hysterically when she saw the picture of Theodora with the Frosty Frizzle.

I picked up the photo of Theodora sitting at the water fountain near the town hall. It made me smile. Theodora *did* look like she was having fun.

Now that I was wearing my eyeglasses it was much easier to read things like the "HAVING A BALL" sign in the photo. In fact, I noticed that there were other things in the photograph that stood out more clearly as well. One thing, in particular, was a clue—a pretty obvious clue as to who might have taken Theodora!

Chapter Nine

ONE, TWO, THREE...

I pointed to the bottom right corner of the photograph. "Do you see that?"

"It looks like a piece of trash or maybe a toy," said Olivia.

"No! Look closely. Where have you seen that design before?" I asked Monica.

"I don't know," Monica shook her head.

"That's a webbed foot just like the webbed foot that belongs to the three-eyed monster on Splinter's skateboard."

"Oh yeah," said Monica. "That does look like part of a webbed foot from Splinter's creepy little monster board."

Olivia's eyes got really big. She slammed the bowl of popcorn she'd been holding down on the floor. The popcorn bounced up in the air and sprinkled all around us. Then she stood and started toward the back door. "I'm going to get him," she said angrily.

"Wait! Take a deep breath and count to three," I said. "Let's think about this for a second. We need a plan."

She paused, knowing I was right. The other girls agreed.

So we put our heads together and devised a plan—a very good plan.

We peeked out the window and noticed that Splinter's skateboard was parked beside the garage just as we hoped it would be.

"OK," said Olivia. "Let's do this!"

We all high-fived each other. Then Olivia and I crept quietly out to the side of the garage. The other girls giggled and watched from the window as we snatched up the skateboard and scurried back inside the house.

We laid the skateboard in the center of the room so that I could snap a picture of it with my dad's camera. Lisa was in charge of uploading the photo to our computer and printing it out.

Meanwhile, Monica drafted a ransom note that said:

"SKATEBOARD FOR THE BEAR." Then we signed it, "The Jumpstart Squad."

"What is a Jumpstart Squad anyway?" asked Lisa.

"I don't know," I answered. "But making up nicknames has always been one of Splinter's *things.*"

We tucked the note and the photo inside an envelope and wrote the word BOOM! on the front of it.

Then we unzipped Monica's large yellow pillow and stuffed the skateboard inside. *He'd never think to look there,* I thought.

The guys in the band were still jamming away when Olivia and I banged on the garage door. Before anyone could answer we dashed back inside the house and spied from the window with the other girls.

Aiden opened the garage door and looked around. He spotted the note lying on the doorstep. He picked it up and slammed the door behind him.

We counted together. "One...two...three..."

All of a sudden, the music stopped. We ducked behind the window and waited.

The garage door swung open again and the Ultimatums band members stepped out.

The girls and I sprinted to the family room and quickly crawled into our sleeping bags.

"Hide yourselves!" I whispered as I slid way down into my sleeping bag and covered my face. I held my breath and listened.

Lisa was in the sleeping bag beside me. She couldn't stop giggling. I peeked out. She looked like a big wiggly inchworm moving around inside her neon-green colored sleeping bag.

The back door slammed. We heard footsteps.

Aiden, Splinter, Bandana and Mike entered the family room.

"OK little Jumpstart girls. Where's Splinter's skateboard?" asked Aiden.

"Yeah," said Splinter. "That's a one-of-a-kind, Brat Monster 360."

I poked my head out from inside my sleeping bag. "You'll get it back when we get our mascot back."

"It's only fair!" shouted Olivia from way inside her sleeping bag.

Splinter grinned as he confessed. "OK, OK, I admit it. I took your cute little Theona. I was just having a little fun with you guys. But I promise I'll give her back to you tomorrow. So now can I *please* have my skateboard back?"

"It's Theodora, not Theona," I said.

"Whatever! Now, tell me where you hid my skateboard."

"Tomorrow," I said. "Come to the pancake breakfast and we'll do an exchange: the skateboard for our mascot!"

Chapter Ten
WHATEVER!

We arrived at the elementary school early the next morning, dressed in our cheerleading outfits. Mrs. Walsh, the cafeteria manager, greeted us at the front door. She flipped on some lights as we followed her down the hallway toward the cafeteria. It felt strange, being at our school on a Saturday morning.

"No skateboarding inside the school," Mrs. Walsh said, noticing the skateboard I was carrying under my arm.

"I'm just holding onto this for someone," I reassured her.

The pancake breakfast was our last attempt to raise the rest of the money we needed for the state competition. We had advertised around town and passed out fliers—a dollar for a plate of pancakes. We all thought that was a pretty good deal. Now all we could do was hope for a good turnout.

Mrs. Walsh assigned us all duties. Dee, Brenna, Lisa and I were in charge of mixing the batter and making the pancakes. Some of the other girls on the squad were responsible for taking orders and collecting the money. Olivia and the rest of the gang were assigned to serving and cleanup duties.

I quickly realized that pancake making wasn't really my thing. I was getting batter everywhere and couldn't seem to flip a pancake correctly if my life depended on it. Mrs. Walsh tried to show me how. She told me I had to wait until bubbles formed on the top of the pancake. So I waited patiently for the bubbles. Then I'd slide my spatula under the pancake. But when I went to flip, that's when it all fell apart. I was creating a big, battery mess.

Knowing I was more of a people person and that my skills would be better served elsewhere, Mrs. Garcia quickly reassigned me to serving and cleanup duties with Olivia and the other girls.

The turnout at the pancake breakfast wasn't bad. The junior and high school football players arrived bright and early to support our cause. They dressed in their uniforms and they all seemed pretty hungry. I figured it was because of all those jumping jacks and laps* around the football field.

Chuck came through the serving line. "Hey Pip. Nice glasses," he said.

I smiled. I'd forgotten I had them on. "Thanks,"

I replied. Then I plopped a pancake on his plate.

Soon after, the high school cheerleaders arrived along with their mascot. At first I wondered how Theo would eat pancakes without having to take off his mascot head. But then I noticed there was a small opening near the mouth of the costume. *He's going to have to cut his pancake into tiny little bites*, I thought.

Someone tapped me on the shoulder. I turned. Sophie was standing beside me with her arms stretched out. "Congratulations on winning at Regionals," she said in an excited, high-pitched tone. She gave me a big squeeze.

Olivia smiled at me, knowing she was next.

"How did you guys do?" I asked.

"We did OK but one of our flyers was injured so we weren't able to do our pyramid stunt."

"That's too bad," said Olivia.

"Yeah, maybe next year," she sighed. Then she spotted Theo. "Gotta go!" she said as she ran over to greet her mascot.

The school cafeteria had filled up in no time. The

football players and cheerleaders occupied an entire section. Soon after, parents and other people from the town had assembled* at the remaining tables. I was passing out pancakes as fast as Brenna, Lisa, Dee and Mrs. Walsh could make them.

Every once in a while I'd glance up at the clock on the wall. I was beginning to worry. There was still no sign of Splinter. *Where was he?*

Olivia appeared to have read my thoughts. "What if he doesn't show up?" she asked me.

"He'll be here," I reassured her, trying to remain positive.

After most of the customers had been served, Olivia and I began our cleanup duties. I grabbed a trash bag and walked from table to table collecting trash.

Mrs. Garcia was sitting at an empty table in the corner counting our earnings. She didn't look very happy as I approached.

"How'd we do?" I asked her.

"Not as well as I had hoped," she sighed. "We're still a little short. It looks like we're going to have to do another fundraiser."

Just then I noticed Splinter entering the cafeteria along with Aiden and Mike. Olivia spotted him, too. I ditched my trash bag and rushed over to greet him. Olivia arrived at the same time and we cornered him near the entrance while Aiden and Mike took off toward the serving line.

"All right little Jumpstart girls, here's your precious little Theona." Splinter reached in his backpack and pulled out our mascot. "Boom!" he said as he slammed the bear into Olivia's hands.

"Her name is Theodora," I corrected him.

"Whatever!" he replied.

Olivia was happy to see Theodora again. She gave her a big kiss and hug.

"Why do you keep calling us that?" I asked.

"What?" he replied.

"Jumpstart girls."

"Oh, that." Splinter laughed. Then he ran his fingers through his spiky brown hair and smiled as though he was *so* very proud of himself. "At the pep rally you girls kinda reminded me of the warm-up band that comes on first at a concert except you're a lot more bouncy. So I decided to nickname you the Jumpstart Squad. The jumpstart is also one of my skateboard moves." He winked. "No one else knows it but me."

"Whatever!" I said as I rolled my eyes.

"So where's my Brat Monster 360 anyway?" he asked.

"Wait here," I said. I ran to the kitchen and opened the janitor's closet. I had hidden it way in the back, behind some cleaning supplies.

I returned quickly with Splinter's Brat Monster 360. "BOOM! Here you go."

"Thanks little Jumpstart girl," said Splinter. Then he bowed and turned away.

As he made his way over to his friends he tapped on his skateboard like it was one of his instruments.

I nodded my head. "That Splinter—what a pain."

"He's more like a thorn," joked Olivia.

Olivia and I were glad to have Theodora back in our possession*. "But now we have another problem," I sighed. I told her what Mrs. Garcia had said about our fundraising.

Olivia looked worried. "The competition is in two weeks. How are we going to raise the rest of the money in time?"

Splinter continued to tap on his skateboard as he socialized* at a nearby table. The tapping suddenly gave me an idea. "I think I know a way to earn the rest of the money," I told Olivia. "But first I need to talk to our coach."

I was on my way across the room to tell Mrs. Garcia my idea when I became sidetracked. A disturbance was brewing* at the high school cheerleaders' table.

Two high school football players were hovering over Theo, taunting him and daring him to take off his mascot head.

"We have a right to know who's under there," joked the shorter kid.

"Yeah," said the taller kid.

Theo rose up from the table and headed toward the door. The two kids followed. Sophie, who'd been sitting beside Theo, got up and ran between them. "Leave him alone," she cried. "If he wants to remain anonymous, that's his right."

The two troublemakers ignored Sophie. They ran around her and darted toward Theo. Theo tried to outmaneuver them. He circled around one of the tables and sprinted toward the exit. But one of the kids blocked him.

They chased Theo around the cafeteria, eventually cornering him by the snack machine.

Chuck realized what was happening and rushed over to defend Theo. "Let him go," he warned.

But the shorter kid paid no attention to Chuck. He grabbed Theo by the shoulders and held him while the taller kid lifted off his mascot head.

The onlookers* gasped when the masked mascot was revealed.

Many of the kids in the cafeteria started laughing. It was a surprise to everyone, including me, when we saw who it was.

The mystery kid underneath the mascot costume was Bandana.

The short kid laughed at Bandana and teased him some more. "What's the matter? Not tough enough to be a real football player?"

"Yeah, guess it's more fun hanging out with the cheerleaders," joked the other kid.

Bandana's face got really red. He ripped the mascot head from the tall kid's grasp and walked toward the exit. Many of the kids were still chuckling and whispering when the cafeteria door banged shut behind Bandana.

I'd never seen Chuck so angry as he moved toward the tall, skinny kid and stood face to face with him so that their noses practically touched.

The next thing I knew, Aiden rushed over and pulled them apart. "It's not worth it," he told Chuck.

Chuck was still mad, but he backed off knowing Aiden was right.

"Bandana can't play sports," he shouted at the two football players.

Aiden gripped Chuck's arm and tried to drag him

68

away.

"He finally found a way to fit in and you took that away from him. I hope you're both happy now!"

Aiden continued to pull Chuck toward the exit.

The two football players stood there—speechless.

The cafeteria door opened and closed again as Chuck and Aiden took off after Bandana.

Chapter Eleven
DO YOUR THING

The purpose of the second pep rally was to get Park Valley psyched up to beat our rival team, the Westland Warriors.

In order to raise the extra money we needed for States I had suggested to Mrs. Garcia that we ask the Ultimatums to play at the rally. This way we could draw a bigger crowd and collect donations while they played.

It took a lot of convincing but the Ultimatums finally agreed to do it. Olivia and I told Splinter that he owed us.

Bandana was the only one who was reluctant* to perform. He was still pretty upset about the pancake breakfast incident. But the guys somehow convinced him to play.

Chuck had known all along that Bandana was the mysterious mascot. In fact, he was the one who told

Bandana about it in the first place. Bandana had always been a big football fan. If he had been able to play football I think he would have, too. Now he wanted nothing to do with the Park Valley Rangers football players. And he no longer wanted to be their mascot. It was a shame because he was so good at it.

Meanwhile, Chuck was back singing with the band. He and Aiden had finally ended their feud* and made up. Aiden realized that he had to let his friend do what he wanted to do, even if it meant that Chuck couldn't spend as much time hanging out with the band.

The second pep rally was about to start. We all stood in the hallway of the high school waiting to go out and perform again. It seemed strange and a little sad not having Theo around to entertain us and keep us calm.

While we waited, we went over our routine. Our squad had made up a new dance to one of the

Ultimatums' songs. It was really cool. Mrs. Garcia also had us working on a more complicated stunt. And because I was in the middle of the pyramid, I was now going to be lifted up even further into a full-extension liberty stunt as opposed to the half-extension pose that I had been doing.

While Olivia and I were stretching, Sophie rushed over to us and handed us a bag.

"What's this?" I asked.

"Get the rest of your squad together and I'll explain," she said.

We huddled in a circle. Then, Sophie told us what we needed to do.

When it was time to go on our squad ran out to the center of the gymnasium and the crowd cheered. The bag that Sophie had handed to us contained yellow bandanas. We had all tied them around our necks before we went on. I looked up and noticed that many people in the audience were wearing bandanas, too.

Everyone stomped and clapped while we introduced the junior football players who were also wearing bandanas around their necks. They ran through our formation as we cheered them on.

STOMP, STOMP, CLAP...Lydon Campbell...

STOMP, STOMP, CLAP...Michael Mann...

Then the high school cheerleaders came out and introduced their football team. Our squad cheered along with them.

STOMP, STOMP, CLAP...Chuck Davis...

To my amazement, every member of the Park Valley football and cheering squad had a bandana tied around their neck.

After all the football players were introduced we continued with the beat.

STOMP, STOMP, CLAP...

Then we began shouting Bandana's name.

STOMP, STOMP, CLAP...BAN-DAN-A

STOMP, STOMP, CLAP...BAN-DAN-A

The high school cheerleading coach carried the mascot costume over to Sophie. The crowd continued to cheer and shout Bandana's name.

It was Olivia's and my job to go and get

Bandana. He was hiding behind his drum set in the right section of the gym, waiting to perform. He seemed a bit confused as Olivia and I walked over, grabbed him by his arms and escorted* him to the center of the gymnasium.

STOMP, STOMP, CLAP...BAN-DAN-A

The crowd continued to chant Bandana's name while Sophie presented the mascot costume to Bandana. He paused for a second. Sophie gave him a "pretty please" look. He shrugged his shoulders and sighed. Then he unzipped the bear costume and stepped into it. Sophie helped him with the mascot head.

The crowd began waving their bandanas in the air as Sophie tied a large bandana around the mascot's neck. Then she gave him a great big bear hug.

The two football players who had teased Bandana at the pancake breakfast approached him. They took turns shaking his big furry hand. It appeared as though they were apologizing.

Then our squad sat in our spot by the

scoreboard and watched as the high school cheerleaders performed first this time. Everyone was cheering and rooting for Bandana as he ran around the gymnasium and did his little dance. When their routine was over, Theo strutted over to the band and picked up his drumsticks.

I'm sure Bandana was happy that he no longer had to keep something that he enjoyed doing a secret. And it was nice to know that all the fans appreciated and supported him.

When the crowd settled down, Mrs. Garcia walked out to the center of the gymnasium and made an announcement. "Let's all give a big round of applause to our Park Valley Rangers junior cheerleaders and wish them well at States!"

Everyone clapped and pounded on the bleachers as our squad stood and ran to get into our positions.

We did a quick cheer. Then the Ultimatums began to play. Chuck walked over to the band and grabbed the microphone. When he started to sing, everyone cheered and waved their bandanas some more. I'd forgotten what a nice-sounding voice he had.

We performed a dance routine to the Ultimatums' newest song called: "Do Your Thing, Do it Well!" At the end of the dance we finished by holding up three signs that, together, read: DO...YOUR...THING!

Afterwards the Ultimatums continued to play while the girls from my squad and I walked around with our cans to collect donations.

Of course, this time we didn't forget about Theodora. She was in a much safer place. Our squad had appointed Monica to be her official guardian during pep rallies and football games.

Monica sat in the front row with Theodora on her lap. She waved Theodora's tiny paw at us. Theodora wore a yellow bandana around her neck and smiled as usual.

Chapter Twelve

OFF TO STATES!

I stood in the school parking lot with my mom, going over the list to make sure I didn't forget anything: Cheerleading outfit? Check... Pompoms? Check... Toothbrush? Check... MP3 player for the *long* bus ride? Check.

My mom wished me luck and told me she and my dad would be there in the morning to watch me perform. I gave her a big hug goodbye and headed over to the bus. *It's amazing how much stuff I need for just one night*, I thought to myself, as I hauled my overnight bag up onto the bus steps and plunked it in the seat beside Lexie.

It was an early Saturday morning. The sun was glaring through the bus driver's window and straight into my eyes. But I didn't mind. It felt good considering the air inside the bus was still very cold from the frost the night before. Even the seats felt cold and stiff as I slid over to the window and tried to get comfortable.

Mrs. Garcia and the other chaperones boarded the bus. "OK girls, settle in. We have a long, three-hour ride ahead of us."

The bus rattled and shook as the driver started up the engine. Everyone cheered and shouted. "States, here we come!" I smiled and waved out the window to my mom as we drove off.

❧ ❧

When I finally stepped off the bus I dropped my overnight bag and stretched my arms and legs. It felt good to be standing again.

"Wow!" said Olivia, admiring the hotel. "I'll bet it's even nicer inside."

It *was* a pretty cool hotel inside. The lobby was gigantic with a big, wide-open area in the center. The rooms on every floor opened up to the main floor below. Lush* green plants surrounded the lobby. In the center were four tall, white trees that reached all the way up to the top floor.

I was going to be sharing a room with Lexie, Brenna and Lexie's mom, Mrs. Moore.

While Mrs. Garcia and a few of the chaperones checked us in, we walked around the hotel with one of the moms to do a little exploring. There was a big indoor pool in the hotel, a game room and even a hot tub. Down the hallway, past the main lobby, was a restaurant. At the entranceway to the restaurant was a round bench with a sculpture of a big fruit bowl in the middle. The restaurant was called Pineapples.

It was a fun-filled day. We swam in the indoor swimming pool and ate at the Pineapples restaurant. But mostly we practiced our routine in a big, empty ballroom. I was still a little nervous about my full-extension liberty stunt. I knew that the judge's eyes would be on me at that point. I'd been working my absolute hardest to get it right. But I was still unsure of myself.

Later that evening, we all got together in Olivia's

room. We curled each others' hair and practiced putting on makeup.

Mrs. Garcia didn't allow us to stay up too late, though. By nine o'clock we were all in our beds—dreaming about the big day ahead of us.

Chapter Thirteen

S–U–C–C–E–S–S

I sat on a bench in the locker room and tied my shoelaces as tight as they would go. It was almost time to go on and I felt revved up inside, like a speedy racecar waiting to take off.

Someone tapped my shoulder. Startled, I looked up.

"Surprise!" said Monica. She leaned over and gave me a big hug.

I jumped up and hugged her back. "How'd you get here?" I asked.

"I came with your mom and dad," she said. "I wanted to surprise you."

I was so very happy to see her. And I had so much to tell her but I knew we didn't have much time. "Meet me afterward," I told her. "We're going to have our pictures taken and I want to get one with you." We squeezed each others' hands and she wished me luck.

Olivia noticed Monica from across the locker room. She rushed over and handed Theodora to her. "We didn't appoint you our official mascot chaperone for nothing," she said.

"Wait! Hold on one more second." Olivia ran back to her gym bag and returned with a handful of bandanas.

She tied a bandana around Theodora's neck and then passed the rest out to the girls on the squad. Monica got one, too. "These bandanas represent the spirit of the Park Valley Rangers cheerleading squad."

We tied the bandanas around our necks and high-fived Monica and Theodora as we raced out of the locker room.

"Let's do this!" we all shouted.

"Go Jumpstart Squad!" yelled Monica as we ran over to our waiting spot.

⸎ ⸎

The brightness of the gymnasium lights made me squint to see the crowd in the stands. I could hear them all as they shouted our team's name. The music was even louder and

I could feel it pulsing* through my body.

So there I was—finally—at that critical moment. Lisa, Brenna and I knew we had to get our pyramid stunt just right in order for our squad to get a high score. I smiled at the judges and concentrated on keeping my movements sharp and clean.

Nicole, Lexie and Dee lifted me up into a full extension. I stretched my arms out into a high-V and held the pose for four counts. Then I readied myself for my dismount, followed by a toe touch. BOOM!...I executed* it perfectly.

I finished with my ending pose and a big smile. I glanced over at Lisa and Brenna. They seemed happy with their performances as well.

Afterward, Mrs. Garcia passed around our scorecard so that we could see how well we did. I needed to run to the locker room and get my eyeglasses from my gym bag in order to read it.

Our marks were pretty high. We received perfect scores for our pyramid stunts and high marks for jumps and overall technique*.

We watched from the stands as the last few squads performed. Then we crossed our fingers while the judges tallied the final scores.

When it was time for the awards ceremony, the judges walked out to the center of the blue mat. They were each holding the trophies that were to be awarded to the top three squads. There was also an award that was given to the team who showed the most spirit.

A judge announced the winners, last to first, while we all stood by nervously. "Third place goes to...the Oakmont Panthers."

There was lots of cheering and clapping as the squad posed with their trophy for a team picture.

"Second place is awarded to...the South Bay Jets.

"The Spirit Award is presented to...the Holliston Hurricanes."

Our team's name hadn't been called. That meant we either got first place or nothing at all. We held each others' hands as the first place winner was announced.

"The first place award goes to...the PARK VALLEY RANGERS!"

We all jumped up and ran to the center of the mat to accept our trophy. Many of the people in the stands stood and applauded loudly as my squad mates and I hugged and gave each other high-fives. Wow! We couldn't believe it. That meant we were going to get to compete at Nationals—the most prestigious* competition in the country.

We were all beaming with happiness as we posed for our winning team photo.

As I was standing there, smiling for the photographer, I suddenly realized I was still wearing my eyeglasses. I started to take them off but then I paused and decided not to. I liked the new me—the one *with* the eyeglasses.

Monica rushed over and congratulated all of us on our victory. "I guess this bear really did bring you guys luck," she said as she handed Theodora back to Olivia.

"Yeah, or maybe it was all that practicing we did," I joked.

My mom and dad were very happy for me. They gave me a bouquet of flowers and big hugs.

Then Monica and I stood side by side and posed for

a photo together.

"Let's get a picture of Theodora with the trophy," I suggested to Olivia and Monica. "That way we can add it to our collection."

Olivia and Monica agreed. We propped Theodora beside the trophy and snapped a photo. *Splinter's gonna love this one*, I thought.

Olivia picked up Theodora and placed her in my hands. "She's yours now. You get to have her," she smiled.

I was confused. "But she was given to you," I said.

"Only for one year, and my year is up. I'm supposed to pass her down to the person on the squad who I feel deserves it the most. And I've chosen you."

I was surprised that Olivia chose me. But she told me that I had so many qualities that she wished she had—like my ability to figure things out and work extra hard to get something right. She also admired the fact that I wasn't afraid to be myself.

"I think you're the perfect cheerleader," said Olivia.

"Thanks. I promise I'll take good care of her," I said as I smiled and squeezed Theodora tight.

Me? Perfect? I didn't really think of myself that way. I guess you could say that being perfect has many different meanings and, after almost a year of being a Park Valley Rangers junior cheerleader I'd developed my own definition of perfect.

To me, being perfect means doing what you like to do and striving to be your very best at it, but also not feeling like you have to be good at everything.

I can't imagine ever being a good softball player. It's just not my thing.

And soccer—that's not really my thing either.

Pancake flipping—perhaps someday my thing, but not right now.

Jumps, flips, dance moves and anything to do with cheerleading—definitely my thing—the thing that taught me a *thing* or two about S-U-C-C-E-S-S.

SUCCESS…VICTORY…JULIET!

Glossary

Many words have more than one meaning. Here are the definitions of words marked with this symbol * (an asterisk) as they are used in sentences.

abrupt (abruptly): *sudden or unexpected*
anonymous: *secret or nameless*
armor: *protective clothing*
assembled: *gathered or came together*
assertive: *confident and forceful*
brewing: *starting to happen*
bronzed: *metallic, shiny, golden brown*
competition: *a contest or challenge*
contentedly: *happily and cheerfully*
critical: *important or key*
dedication: *loyalty and dependability*
dislodge: *to free or remove*
disqualified: *removed from a contest*
escorted: *led, guided or walked along with*
etched: *carved*

92

executed: *performed or carried out*

feud: *an argument or quarrel that's been going on for a long time*

formation: *position or arrangement of the team to get ready for a cheer activity*

fundraising: *raising money for a good cause*

halt: *stop or finish*

hip-hop: *a dance performed to a popular style of music that includes rap*

hovering: *hanging around, staying nearby*

incorporating: *adding or including something new*

indications: *signs or hints*

keyboard: *a piano-like musical instrument, often electric*

laps: *sprints or runs*

lush: *full and leafy*

Nationals: *a competition* where cheerleading squads from every state in the country come together to compete*

oblivious: *unaware or not paying attention*

occupied: *took up or used a certain space*

onlookers: *people watching something*

panicky: *jumpy or alarmed*
possession: *owning or having something*
prestigious: *important and valuable*
pulsing: *pounding, vibrating or beating*
quest: *mission or search*
Regionals: *a competition* where cheerleading squads from a group of leagues come together to compete*
reluctant: *unwilling or unsure*
reminisced: *looked back in time or remembered the past fondly*
reserved: *held onto or saved*
retrieve: *recover or take back*
slung: *hanging off of or placed around something*
socialized: *spoke to or mixed with others*
States: *a competition* where cheerleading squads from different regions within a state come together to compete*
strutted: *proudly walked or marched*
technique: *method or way of performing a skill*
unison: *all together or at the same time*
varsity: *the main squad that represents a school or upper class*

94

Cheerleading Chants and Cheers
Try Some Cheers of Your Own

The Success Cheer:
(where you see dashes, spell the word)
S-U-C-C-E-S-S
That's the way we spell SUCCESS
V-I-C-T-O-R-Y
VICTORY, VICTORY—that's our cry
R-A-N-G-E-R-S
RANGERS, RANGERS—we're the best
S-U-C-C-E-S-S
SUCCESS...VICTORY...RANGERS!

The Winning Cheer:
We are the Rangers
And we're here to say
We're going to help our team win today
We may be new
We may be green
But we're going to be part
Of the winning team!

Everywhere We Go:

Cheerleaders: Everywhere we go-oh
Crowd (echo): Everywhere we go-oh
Cheerleaders: People want to kno-oh
Crowd (echo): People want to kno-oh
Cheerleaders: Who we are
So we tell them
We are the Rangers
Crowd (echo): We are the Rangers
Cheerleaders: The mighty, mighty Rangers
Crowd (echo): The mighty, mighty Rangers
Goooo Rangers!

Ready Set:

Ready set
You bet
Got the spirit
Got the might
Got the power-to-succeed
So here we go
We're gonna show
We've got the best-team-in-the league
Gonna fight
With all our might
To prove we're dynamite!

Basic Chant:

Go...
Fight...
Win Tonight
Go-Fight-Win-Tonight!

About the Author

Julie Driscoll keeps a notebook with her at all times because everywhere she goes, something funny or exciting happens that she knows would make for an interesting story.

Her greatest inspirations are her two daughters, Emily and Kerry and her husband, Steve, who's a lot like a little kid trapped inside a grown-up's body.

Mrs. Driscoll is a writer and artist. She has written a screenplay in the family genre and a television pilot for a local network.

*In addition to **The Jumpstart Squad**, Mrs. Driscoll has written three other books in the Our Generation® Series, **Adventures at Shelby Stables**, **The Note in the Piano** and **Blizzard on Moose Mountain**.*

A special thanks from the author to the following people:

The Methuen Rangers Junior Cheer Squad
The Milton Broncos Junior Cheer Squad
Kasey and Caroline Sullivan
Adrianna Lemieux
Monica Woods
Megan Casey